ETHICAL NECROMANCY

ETHICAL NECROMANCY

NEW YORK | LOS ANGELES

Jacket design by @schism.art (Instagram)

Jacket Copyright © 2024 by Winding Road Stories

Interior Design by Winding Road Stories

ISBN#: 978-1-960724-36-6 (pbk)
ISBN#: 978-1-960724-37-3 (ebook)

Published by Winding Road Stories

www.windingroadstories.com

To healing

IN THE GARDEN

Sɪɴᴇ́ᴀᴅ Pᴀʟᴍᴇʀ ɪꜱ ꜱɪᴄᴋ.

Everyone knows that Sinéad Palmer is sick; it's as much a constant as the sun rising and setting or teenagers smoking weed behind the bleachers during track meets or Damon Miller (*Artie and Frances' boy*, older folks always clarify when discussing him) hitting deer head-on with his shitty blue pickup. Weavewool, if nothing else, is a town of constants.

Sinéad Palmer has been sick for a long time:

1. **She had always been a frail girl, too-ashy skin, too-limber form, too many absences from elementary school.**
2. **She was terrified of most things, including and especially other people. This has led to her becoming a bit of a ghost story in town; her family was rather wealthy, due to the grace of God or perhaps the death of a cousin, so it was easy to gossip about the Palmers without shame.**
3. **Seven months ago, a blood vessel ruptured in her brain and she found herself dead. Six months ago, she found herself covered in dirt, significantly *less* dead.**

The miraculous undeath of Sinéad Palmer was gossiped about in town for about two weeks until that rascal CJ Sawyer stole some runic tomes from the high school's pitiful excuse of a collection, after which the gossip moved on, as it always did.

Today, Sinéad Palmer is venturing out of her home, an action that she is kind of proud of. A little bit proud of. Not *too* proud of, because taking pride in such bland things can feel a little bit pathetic. And, of course, her mother's voice chides her in her head. Pride is a sin—a deadly one, at that.

(Sinéad has sometimes wondered if--regarding fatality, mostly, but also just generally—sins are worse than sickness. She's also sometimes wondered if sins and sicknesses are the same things. She wrote that down in her diary when she was fourteen and then she burned the page an hour later upon rereading it, putting the ashes under the azalea bushes because her teenage melancholy made her want to run into the ocean. She has returned to this thought often of late, even though she doesn't really *want* to return to it. She's a grown woman, after all, and not the type of grown woman who fixates on her years-old angst until it suffocates her.)

Getting dressed is the first effort out of many. Sinéad doesn't care much for it—she is so tired, so often, and these things, sweaters and skin and bones, are so heavy to wear. Still, she slips into her body, and then she slips the body into clothes. It hurts to be alive, she has to remember every single time. She ought to be grateful, she thinks.

Sinéad walks to a drug store called Pill's Pills, as it is owned by George Pill, an old man with superglued glasses, a raspy voice, and a penchant for swearing very loudly at the night sky from the roof of his house. The store is dusty and walking into it makes the air feel Atlas-heavy, a depressing scene; the waxy floors are a sickly yellow-gray, and the lightbulbs are flickering more often than not. Annie (who works Monday-Tuesday-Wednesday evenings and Saturday-Sunday mornings—Sinéad times her ventures accordingly) says it's because the building is old and full of spite. Annie says a lot of things like this because Annie likes to personify every single thing that she can. It makes her life a little bit easier, probably.

Annie is on her phone behind the register. She had barely even reacted to the bell at the entrance; she's so absorbed in her little solitaire game. But eventually, her face twitches, and, still not looking up, she says, "Hey, Nadie," in her strange little songbird drawl. She puts her phone in her jeans pocket (a small hole in the bottom from where she used to keep her lighter), turns around and smiles. She's got crooked teeth and freckles, and her wheat-colored eyes have deep-dark circles under them.

Annie studied alchemy in college, which is very impressive on paper, but doesn't lead to much in the realm of proper employment unless you're willing to compromise your moral code. She often complains about this to Sinéad, saying, I mean, I think it's a consequence of the whole We Need More Women In SSTEM movement; they have too many fucking women in SSTEM.

(Sinéad will sometimes counter this with, well, sorcery programs are still so white-male-dominated, you *know* this. Don't blame other women. Annie counters this with *I'm* not blaming other women, *society* is. That transmutation firm in Richmond had, like, five open positions, and they considered me a candidate for the one *diversity hire*. And Annie would roll her eyes, and Sinéad would concede that this is fair.)

Memories aside, this visit is happening for a reason. So, Sinéad starts with, "Hello, how are you?" which causes Annie to roll her eyes and go through the canvas bag she keeps right by the register, pulling out a mason jar wrapped in brown paper and tied with a red piece of twine. Sinéad nods, "Thanks."

Annie nods. "Any new growth?"

"New kind of mushroom," Sinéad offers and filters through her jean pocket for it. It's pink, and it glows in the dark. Annie grins and squeezes the cap, and the mushroom *bleeds*. "I'm not comforted by that growing on my body," Sinéad notes, "if it does that."

"Okay, but it has some pretty cool properties, like, for... alchemy stuff. Not hallucinogenic, though, which is a bummer."

Here is a list of things Annie has called a "bummer," per Sinéad's memory:

1. **Her car running out of gas while she was driving to her uncle's wake.**
2. **The very concept of Valentine's Day.**
3. **Aaron Toledo's reanimated cat not meowing in the same tone that it did when it was alive.**
4. **Sinéad failing chemistry back when they were in high school.**
5. **A mushroom that grew on Sinéad's still-living corpse not being as hallucinogenic as past mushrooms.**

This is to say that Annie's use of the word *bummer*, right there,could mean a lot of things. Sinéad sighs and asks, "Is that my blood?" to which Annie responds, "No, it's just a mushroom thing. Just because it's growing on your body doesn't mean it's *you*, y'know? These little guys just bleed." And she does a little shaking gesture with the mushroom cap, the bloody ooze splashing all over her fingers. She places the cap into a small bag and then pulls out a small container of hand sanitizer, the kind with glitter in it.

Sinéad takes the jar Annie had handed her, buys some gummy worms, and leaves; she listens to the bell at the door ring and ring and ring. Her bones hurt. People stare at her as she walks by, which is reasonable. She hates stares, but she is used to them because stares are a reasonable reaction to a dead woman walking. There aren't too many cases of successful full-form necromancy, especially not in a town like Weavewool, so Sinéad has resigned herself to a life of discomfort and whispers from teenagers who are too scared to ask her questions.

The issues with being alive again are:

1. **Sinéad, always quiet and unobtrusive, now feels as if she is always loud and obtrusive, even though she hasn't changed very much at all.**
2. **She does not feel like herself all of the time, especially not in her body; she prefers to be just her ghost, floating around and entirely hers, rather than mycelium networks whispering inside of a corpse along *with* her. She wants a quiet life. She cannot have one.**
3. **She didn't ask to be brought back to life, to begin with.**

Regardless. Sinéad arrives back home, feeds the cat, unwraps the mason jar to reveal a familiar, burnt-smelling balm. She puts a little dab on her pointer finger and licks it, wincing at the taste. It's not supposed to be eaten, of course, but Sinéad is always tempted, in the same way that she is tempted to touch candle flame or stare at the sun. (Another advantage of ghosthood is that she can do both of those things without consequence, but she is trying to commit to having a body for now, so she'll have to hold back on her usual small indulgences.)

She goes to her room; checks her email. Her inbox is spam, mostly: your account has been hacked, here's where to buy potions that make your dick bigger, here's a nonsense combination of letters and a link to a website. But there's one email that does catch her eye—

From Loamclay Undeath Society
<contact@loamclayundeath.org>
to *nadiepalmer*
Subject: Potential interview
Ms. Palmer,

We here at the **Loamclay Undeath Society** (based in Violet Beach, MD) were alerted of your current state by a former academic advisor of one Ms. Anne Freeman and were curious as to whether we could get a firsthand account of your experience. Our organization is centered on documenting the experience of undeath (and resurrection, necromantic reanimation, *et al.*), and your experience would be illuminating, particularly as your revival was—apparently—orchestrated through bioarcane compounds rather than typical hemoarcane means.

We also offer **support** for the undead (resurrected, reanimated, et al.), and are at the forefront of **ethical necromantic research**—a subject we're sure you know is oft-ignored, even in sorcery circles! We want to help you, and we hope you're willing to help us.

Regards,

Dr. M. Stone, Ph.D.

Therapist

Loamclay Undeath Society

(to contact me personally, email *marastone@loamclayundeath.org*)

Sinéad blinks dumbly at the text, rereading it over and over. At the top of the email there is a colorful header, animated to look like clouds passing by the setting sun, with the name of the society in bold, all-caps lettering, as well as a phone number and an address. She clicks reply, types out, *I'm willing to speak with your people, though for the details, you ought to contact Ms. Freeman.* She gives her phone number, adds some pleasantries, sends it and worries she used far too many exclamation points in the pleasantries. So, to avoid these worries, she shuts the computer and gets her sketchbook, grabs charcoal, and takes a benzo, because panic is bad and she can feel it rushing up behind her whenever she thinks of anything. She pictures her panic tackling the spirit out of her.

She draws her plants, and she draws Annie. Annie has a nice face to draw, and there's the image, imprinted, of one night in the garden, eyes too wide and teary. A face for silence and being held. By the earth, by Annie, by both at once. Annie was covered in dirt. Annie was beautiful. Annie smelled like battery acid and maraschino cherries. But Sinéad can't draw that smell, so instead, she draws Annie's face as it was today, sleepy and smug. Sinéad smiles as she finishes it and folds the paper into tiny fractions of its size, tucking it into a drawer full of similarly folded pages. On the next page of her sketchbook, she starts sketching lilies.

Here is a list of other things Annie looked like that night:

1. **Like she had just run a marathon.**
2. **Like there was light spilling out of her veins and arteries and into the earth.**
3. **Like she'd just done something terribly wrong but also something wonderful. These things are hard to explain.**

Sinéad draws herself a bath, with bubbles that smell like lavender. The water scalds her skin, but that's okay; nerve endings and hyphae alike scream *hot!* at her, which is kind of funny. Not ha-ha, more nodding in acknowledgement. The nerves shouldn't work and the hyphae ought to be in the ground, talking to things that are more like themselves rather than just the remains of a dead girl. She sinks into the hot water, letting the lavender take her. She feels more like a garden because of that—an apology to the fungi, maybe, for the aforementioned sin of being undead. Sinéad briefly considers, if she were still a churchgoer, what she would say in the confession booth:

1. **My last confession was five years ago. I died and a friend brought me back using sorcery, but I swear, I'm, uh, hate the sin, love the sinner with that sort of thing. I would never do it myself, Father. Now, my body is wrong, and I'm not always inside of it, but I don't want to die again. I remember it hurting. Dying, I mean.**

(There are a lot of lies in this one, which is also a sin. But Sinéad won't bring that into this. Guilt eats her alive so much that it hardly makes a difference anymore.)

2. **My last confession was yesterday, to myself, in my bedroom mirror. Sometimes this feels messianic, I rose from death and**

here I am. What penance need I pay before I make my grand return to heaven? I will need someone to feed my cat.

(This one is mostly a joke.)

3. My last confession was a lifetime ago. My body is not my own. My body is supposed to be in the dirt. I don't think I can fix this with Hail Marys or praying the rosary or or or or or or—

(This is when she submerges herself completely in the water, a distraction, because panic makes the ghost less stable. Apparently. Annie gave a whole speech on this early on, but Sinéad did not pay attention because there was a lot of jargon that she didn't know; all of that magic stuff never clicked with her. Sinéad lets the water consume her briefly and ignores the fact that she'll need to rinse the bubbles from her hair after this, which is frustrating, an overall unpleasant sensation for the senses.)

Sinéad pokes her head out to take a breath. The bath has flooded over onto the floor. She sighs, turns off the tap, retrieves the jar of balm from the edge of the tub. She rubs the balm on her stomach, on her chest, on her forehead. It is remarkably cold-feeling, giving her goosebumps all up her arms, tiny fungi rising out of them as if to say hello. She feels sick, but she feels more awake, too. Annie says this balm is for reminding the body that it's alive and that it ought to do the work of being alive. Sinéad thinks it serves this purpose very well, but she doesn't really want to know what's inside of it.

She spends her afternoon in the bath, letting herself be buried once more until the water goes cold, after which the tub is drained, and the floor is left flooded.

She makes a frittata for dinner. She eats it. She puts leftovers into a Tupperware and puts that Tupperware into the fridge. She pets the cat, who bumps his head at her shins whenever she tries to move away from him. She goes to sleep, sending Annie a text before closing her eyes completely. She types:

1. hey! jsyk, got an email from a nec organization today that mentioned an advisor of yours & you; i gave them your number.

Which she deletes before sending. She tries again, erases that, and sends her third attempt before she can think any further about it.

2. got an email from the loamclay undeath society today. they want to interview me. they might call you? hope you're alright. rest well. <3

3. heard from the loamclay undeath society; you know anything about them? thanks for the jar, really woke me up. goodnight!

Sinéad proceeds to fully encase herself in blankets and drift off. She does not dream, because she doesn't do that sort of thing anymore. There are frantic whispers, of course, *grow-grow-grow*, but that is just the nature of rotting. It is kind of comforting, by now, a sort of white noise in the back corners of her brain. The blankets smother her, strangle her, but she keeps on breathing and hates herself for every second of it.

A new day rises. Sinéad stretches, hears her bones click against each other too loud. She feeds the cat, who sleeps on her bed, now, because he's getting so-very-spoiled. (Death made Sinéad *soft*, she complains to no one because she doesn't enjoy talking to very many people and it seems terribly ungrateful to complain about such silly things. Or anything at all, really.) She puts on clothes; she breathes. Her phone is dead, because she forgot to plug it in, so she plugs it in and sighs, goes to make breakfast. Instant oatmeal. Cinnamon. Sugar. Blueberries.

More sugar. It's not like it'll kill her any faster.

Well. She's not so sure of that.

Here is what Annie said right after she woke Sinéad Palmer from death:

1. **Oh my God. Holy shit. Okay—I didn't write any of my processes down, fuck, but, *Sinéad.* Nadie, you're. Wow.**
2. **I'm really sorry.**
3. **I'm so, so sorry.**
4. **I couldn't handle the thought of you dead, Nadie.**
5. **I love you.**
6. **Do you forgive me?**
7. **Oh, shit, your vocal cords might take a little bit to heal, actually. We can talk later about that.**

(It is important to note that the two of them never talked later about forgiveness or apologies. Sinéad didn't think it was appropriate. They discussed other topics, however, in great, stuttering detail.)

8. **Holy shit, I can't believe it worked. Look, I don't know how long this will last, Nadie, I just.**

(Annie was quiet after that. She was quiet for hours, pacing around the piles of dirt, knees and hands covered in detritus, apologies muffled by silent, fuzzy sobs. Sinéad remembers mostly feeling nauseous that day and feeling like something, like her *self* was wrong. She also remembers that her mother had buried her in a terribly ugly dress, which she is angry at her younger sister for allowing.

The last point in Annie's little post-ritual monologue remains the most important. I don't know how long this will last. Annie *still* doesn't know how long this will last. They keep going about their days, checking in with messages or visits to the store or always-awkward sleepovers or what have you. And they keep the story simple. Sinéad Palmer is sick. This is true. She is sick. She died of being sick and it's not like the sick ever left her body. Sinéad Palmer is sick, and she is dead of sickness, and she is alive all the same.

(Sometimes, Annie says, I wish I could make it so it wasn't so miserable, and Sinéad rolls her eyes and says, You don't owe me anything else. Annie says, It's not about owing. If it was about owing, I'd give you a lot more than just medicine. She laughs. And Sinéad blinks, and she says nothing, because what the hell has she ever done for Annie?)

(Annie says, You listen. You always listen.)

Birds chirp from the garden. Wrens, mostly. She watched a video about birdcalls, once. Thinking it would be a nice distraction. It gave her a migraine, the dull pain of which returns when she thinks too hard on the memory. Birds are just terribly noisy creatures, really. Not that loudness is wrong, it's just… overwhelming.

Sinéad decides that she needs to work on the garden soon. She likes the garden, she belongs in it. She wasn't ever much of a gardener before this, but now, it's a way to feel calm, feel grounded. Sometimes, she fantasizes about digging a new hole and just living there. But that would be inappropriate.

There is a familiar buzz: Sinéad's phone turning on from the windowsill it is sat on. She closes her eyes, tries to calm herself. The prospect of emails, voicemails, text messages, and the like is a horrifying thing. She doesn't know why she is so often full to the brim with dread, but she doesn't think it's a curable condition. Annie's brother once said that maybe the mushrooms were making her crazy, and Sinéad really, really wishes that this were true, but she was crazy in this particular regard long before she was mostly made of decomposing matter.

The notifications on Sinéad's phone are as follows:

1. **Message from** *Annie Freeman* ♡: **LUSMD reached out to me as well—they do good work AFAIK. I'm gonna at least do a phone intervi…**

2. **Message from** *Bryony Palmer*: **mom's being insane again. locked me out of new apartment just as a warning. blocked your n…**

3. **Message from** *Annie Freeman* ♡: **You don't need to do the same of course! All about your comfort on the matter**

4. Email - *marastone@loamclayundeath.org* - Following up! - **Hi, Sinéad. It's Dr. Stone, from the Loamclay Undeath Society. Attached is a list of times...**

Sinéad lets out a long, hearty breath and sets her phone down. The screen is cracked in a way that slices her finger if she holds the device the wrong way. She learned to stop holding it as such after she ran out of the Band-Aids with little flowers on them which Pill's Pills doesn't sell anymore.

She wants to garden, so she goes and gardens. The cat has already found his way into a sunny spot by the window, so she pets him as she exits. Everything is starting to look lovely, especially considering it was completely turned over a few months back. There are daffodils, here for spring and hopeful in their screaming yellowness, and she lets her eyes focus on them. Her body falls to its knees. She feels the dirt on her bare hands and smiles at the gentle cold of it.

She wants to say, *I was here too, once*, to the flowers, as she pats the ground gently. But that is not the type of thing she would say out loud. Roy, next door, with the beerbelly and the too-bright blue eyes and the wrinkles, has horrifyingly good hearing, and he's been looking for reasons to get Sinéad out of here ever since she became the sole proprietor of her little house and its little garden. He has liked her even less over these last few months because he finds her state to be unnatural and ungodly. So, if he heard her say such a thing, she would be called crazy or sent away or something like that. She's not sure of the ethics of institutionalizing the revived, because she's—quite deftly—managed to avoid the thought so far.

(Her mother had her check into a treatment center when she was sixteen after a particularly embarrassing-to-the-family panic attack, and even all these years later she still bristles at the thought of that sterile ward and the too-friendly nurses. She remembers that some kid drew arcane runes during art-therapy-hour and the whole floor had to be evacuated because of the resulting fires. She had stood in a puddle in the hospital parking lot in socked feet and baggy clothes and kind of envied the kid's guts.)

Anyway, she's dug a hole in the garden, she's digging a hole in the garden. She hears her phone ringing from inside. It's Annie; it's always Annie.

"You doing alright?" because Annie-calls always start with this. Her voice is gentle, lilting, and always painfully genuine.

"The balm helped."

"I meant in your brain. You seemed out of it yesterday. I was worried!" and she stops talking there, waits for Sinéad's response.

"I'm trying to commit to not just ghosting."

Ghosting is Annie's verb, originally, for the particular phenomenon of Sinéad letting her spirit drift out of the corpse. This is:

1. **Comfortable—there are no heavy weights, nor are there eyes on her.**
2. **Easy—it takes a lot of energy to be alive when you ought not to be.**
3. **Sustainable—so long as the cat is fed, Sinéad doesn't have to do anything at all. Well. She still has to *think*, and it's harder to *think*, but sometimes that's alright, too. She can be kind of thoughtless, and there's so much pleasantness in that.**

"I'm really proud," Annie says, "It's a big step for you. I know you didn't really ask for this, but. What I'm trying to say—" the *g* in *trying* dropped, so she's nervous; Sinéad can read Annie easily enough; it's been so many years of knowing her and observing her and wanting to be held by her and wanting to hold her in return.

Sinéad cuts her off before things get too strange: "I'm kinda... thanks. Yeah. I'll join you in... in interviewing. Or whatever."

"You don't have to. And I won't either if you don't want me to."

"Nah, uh, I want to help you get your name out there. Maybe it'll get you money. Or job offers, at least. You deserve that. You're... you work miracles. You know."

"I worked *a* miracle. Singular. And you did most of the work. By dying, and then not dying. It's a lot about," lower-pitched and anxious, "it's about the connection you have with the being you're getting back up. And, well..." with a joking wink attached.

"I know, yeah. Look, I'm, uh, working in the garden today, so I can't talk. But. You know, I know, we both know."

"Yeah." And she can imagine Annie smiling over the phone, toothy. Maybe the sunlight catches in those shiny baubles she puts in her braids. A halo. Sinéad scolds herself. That's stupid. Annie chimes in again, "I'll let you go!"

She puts the phone down and sighs. The trowel beckons. She digs several holes of varying sizes, and nods at them with respect, planting bulbs in a few of them. She eats the leftover frittata. She puts on pajamas. She feeds the cat. She watches the news. She draws the cat and shows off her handiwork to him. He meows, apathetic. She sends an email confirming a phone interview. She goes to bed.

Dr. Mara Stone calls her at nine AM sharp the next morning. Her spine cracks as she rolls over in bed to pick up her phone, every individual vertebra screaming at her. She gets the phone anyway, rolls back over in bed as the lines connect.

Dr. Mara Stone has a slow voice, foggy and embracing. She is very polite, and she listens so clearly that it's like Sinéad can hear her nodding her head, squinting her eyes, pushing the round-silver-spectacles-with-the-chain from the photos up her nose. After formalities, however—medical history pre-revival, personal and professional basics, and the like—she begins to ask questions that Sinéad did not prepare answers for. Among others:

1. What emotions does being undead inspire in you?

(Confusion. Relief. I'm alive. That's good. I am sometimes anxious about the passage of time. I experience depressive symptoms, but this is not new. I am not very good at explaining my feelings. Um. I'm sometimes grateful. Sometimes angry. I have feelings about it in the same way that I used to have feelings about being alive.)

2. Do you behave differently than you did prior to death?

(I am less active. Physical activity is very difficult. Oftentimes I like to sit outside of my body and simply exist as a spirit. My sister is allergic to the spores that it's made of, though, so I have to avoid it when she visits. She's seventeen. And then, uh, Ms. Freeman and I are close. We were close before, old friends, but I spend more time with her now. We began a thing. Well. You know. And I spend more time in the garden.)

3. Do you find yourself wanting to return to the earth?

(...On occasion?)

There are more questions, which Sinéad kind of blacks out for. Prior talent with anything arcane (none), pain in the head due to cause of death (limited), living situation (recently changed because her mother couldn't stand being in a house with a corpse). Boring things, boring questions, boring answers, a tiny stomachache. Then technical things, mechanical questions, gross answers, and a larger stomachache.

Dr. Mara Stone thanks Sinéad for her honesty, and then says, "These things can be very difficult, emotionally. I know this. I am glad that you have a support network in Ms. Freeman, but if you want to speak to me again, I am perfectly willing. We also have on-site providers if you're ever in the area."

Sinéad says, "Maybe."

She goes into town to visit Annie; they grab coffee. They discuss the interview, which Annie takes notes on. Annie also takes the drawing of the cat and laughs at it, delighted, says she'll put it on her bedroom wall. Sinéad blushes. Annie starts rambling about an idea she had for an alchemical community garden that she's going to go to city hall about. Sinéad nods, fascinated not only by Annie's passion but also by the moss that grows on the concrete side of this cafe. She imagines it growing toward her, climbing up her and covering her.

The two of them visit Annie's apartment because Annie's housemate is on a work trip. They have themselves a pleasant afternoon—a few episodes of a sitcom that Sinéad has never seen before, and sex. The sex is nice—Sinéad was never the type to have a high libido, fatigue and antidepressant side-effects ruling her mind for most of her brief adult life; death-then-undeath has actually made the act more enjoyable than it ever was in life.

(Annie is also, as she is with most things, terribly good at it, silly and kind and soft, damn quick with her tongue and intimately aware of Sinéad's... everything in a way that nobody else could be. Sinéad lets herself moan, lets herself enjoy it, lets herself touch Annie and feel something wonderful, for once.)

The two of them laugh, and they spoon—Sinéad, in spite of her height, finds herself curled up, body too cold and bones too sharp to be bigger. Annie says, "I'm glad you're back. I'm glad we can do this." Sinéad hums a response, passive. Annie continues, "It's pretty stupid to say this immediately after going down on you, but I really hope you can forgive me."

"I do," Sinéad says, "It's hard, but I do. It's not like you could've, uh, you could've asked, or anything." She rolls over to face Annie. "I'm happy I get to be with you this time around. It's a nice sort of, you know, a nice second chance."

"You don't need to forgive me." Annie's eyes are intense, pupils still a little bit blown-wide. "I wouldn't forgive me. I never even asked you—"

"But I do." Sinéad touches Annie's face and immediately feels guilty about it, because that might make the situation more awkward, stilted. Annie's eyes close, and she leans into the touch just a bit. "Sometimes I'm angry. Never at, uh, never at you. My body and the dirt, that's what I'm angry at. Not you, just. Other stuff."

"You should be angry at me, too," Annie says, voice much graver than Sinéad is used to or comfortable with, and then, "Nadie, do you want to go back?"

And Sinéad doesn't respond to that, just kisses Annie hard, with too much teeth and tongue involved. Annie had reapplied her ChapStick at some point, and it tastes like strawberries.

The two of them redress themselves and pretend that the prior conversation doesn't exist, that it never existed. This is the furthest such a talk has ever gotten, after all. It's a terrifying conversation to have. Sinéad wishes they could forget to have it, that they could keep forgetting to have it, and that the strangeness of it would disappear, and she and Annie could forget everything about the undeath except for each other. Sinéad wishes she didn't think so much, and so often; she wishes she were more alive or maybe more dead, just something less in-between.

Sinéad goes home, feels a lingering dread surrounding her and swaddling her with every step inside of the house. There is something comforting in that. She is not sure what.

She makes instant ramen for dinner, and she feeds the cat. She draws a body covered in moss. She pins it to her bedroom wall. She sleeps.

She wakes up sore and dreamless as ever. She spends two hours on her back, staring at the ceiling.

And she decides to go out into the garden.

She digs more holes:

1. **This hole is small. Fit for seeds, maybe a small bulb.**
2. **This hole connects to that one, goes deeper.**
3. **This hole goes deeper. Sinéad puts her leg inside of it.**
4. **This hole makes the other holes, the entire hole, wider. The other leg. She is standing in a hole now. It is comfortable, the soil cool from recent rainfall and morning dew.**
5. **She digs deeper.**
6. **She digs deeper.**
7. **She digs deeper.**

It is dark here, and it is comfortable, and she imagines burial. Dirt on skin, cool and damp; a slow sensation of freezing. She wasn't awake the first time, but she imagines it to be an interesting experience. Healing, even. Returning to the earth. Annie said that there was a lot of embalmment going on, the first time, which is less interesting, less healing, less returning to the earth. Annie needed a lot of blood to bring her back.

Dirt surrounds her. She lets it. She places the trowel above her. It is sundown. She began before noon. Time flies, she supposes. She lets the hyphae fall into roots, into other living-things, and it's comfortable. She becomes the dirt; the dirt becomes her. She is in the garden and she is the garden. This is a pleasant image; snowdrops growing all over her, ivy crawling over her legs and stomach and spine and breasts and neck and arms and face and and and and and.

She exhales, eyes closed. She inhales dirt and dirt only, starts to choke, and—

She tries to exhale, and she tries to open her eyes, and she tries to crawl as dirt follows her, and worms crawl, and roots feel like chains, suddenly.

Here is a collection of split-second-long thoughts that Sinéad Palmer considers using for her *final* thought, her grand finale, her exit from this mortal plane the second time over:

1. This is what I deserve.
2. At least it's six months more than I was supposed to get.
3. I wanted this.
4. I'm drowning, I'm drowning, I'm drowning.
5. Someone needs to feed the cat his dinner.
6. Annie.

These thoughts run wild around her brain, and her spirit won't leave and let her out, and she feels the mushrooms and the dirt growing and growing as she struggled, so she stops struggling, and—

A hand, offered.

A hand, given.

Sinéad is pulled up, and she is held, and she is told that this is an impulse that needs to be studied, but mostly, she is just held. She exhales, she exhales, she exhales, and Annie does not let go of her as she does.

The dirt on her shoulders feels heavy, but the night ahead (sky welcoming it with pink and gold to celebrate) does not. Sinéad exhales once more.

She'd like to stay here, she thinks. She could stay here forever.

Three Postcards From Something New

Today I became. I was in the dirt and then I wasn't. My legs and arms are long and sturdy and they sing loud like chimes when I step and move. To become and especially to become something new, it takes a lot of work! The sun and the sky eat at you and I had to learn quickly how not to be eaten. My nails are full of earth and iron and that is a heavy, heavy burden. But I am strong and I don't want to complain! My becoming is an honor and a blessing and I can't give up this sort of opportunity. I miss you and I love you very much.

—◆—

The second one has that same bird, perched delicately on a cartoonishly autumnal branch. The thin white border around the painting has dirt or maybe tea or coffee staining the lower left corner. The stamp is one with blocky-inked, red flowers.

Back before I was new, I spent a long time waiting for it. There were too many things crawling to call it stasis, but I was still and I was very good at being still. I was spinal fluid and blood fermenting and now I am something closer to mead. When I was old, people called me honey, so I think it makes sense that I'd become mead next. Don't you?

I have never had mead. I heard about it in stories and saw it written down, and I know what it is because it's a pretty, pretty word. It adds romance, it adds complexity. I am sweetness and patience all wrapped up! I have learned not to be eaten, but God knows I can't stop anyone from drinking me. I am not a storyteller, but I wish I were; I want to build something from all of this. But I am just liquid and mud, and I can live with that! I want to fill spaces. I want to be the shape of the world around me. Write back soon!

———◆———

The third one is a snowy scene, birdless save for long brown lines scattered far back that, if squinted at, resemble feathers. The stamp is placed slightly off—it's gone diagonal, and the outlines of the square it's supposed to fit into show through. The stamp itself has a tennis racket on it.

When you saw me, you were so scared that I got scared too, and I'm sorry. I thought you'd read my letters, but I found the shreds of them on the sidewalks near your house. You said I am gone and that I am lying to you and I wish that were true, because then I wouldn't have to make you see me again. I don't want to force you to do anything, but I need to be seen. I can't trust anyone with all this dirt on me but you.

I know I am new now, but parts of me want to be something old instead. I crawled out of dirt with every bone yelling with want for the old, and sometimes they still yell.

I will see you again, and again, and again.

A House That Cannot Love You

THE HOUSE IS A comfortable one, twobeds twobaths, with dark, damp wooden floors that threatened to mold. You can't call their bluff much longer. There is green outside, big and crawling and pretty. It probably was a patch of flowers, once, or maybe a vegetable patch, but now it's just green all the way down. Really, you prefer it that way. You don't have the skills for upkeep, and the house seems to like it, anyway.

You have been in this house longer than you can remember. Of course, you don't have very much to remember. You weren't, and then you were. You used to have a body, but you don't anymore. Now, you have the house.

You go about your days pleasantly and without much worry. You examine the walls, the broken glass of the third window. You worry whenever things are out of place—new glass shards or leaves that blow in from the outside. But, you numbered the windows early on in your time here, and you've developed a very good system for looking at them. The third one is your favorite. You like the shape of its big missing piece, the thin cracks that extend out from around it like veins. It's always been like this. Sometimes, you like to think about what broke it. Probably a rock, but maybe a bird or a bullet or a lovers' quarrel. The house certainly doesn't remember, so you don't try to remember it either. It's fun to tell stories, though.

After the third window, you look at the others—seven next, then nine, then eleven, then six, then five, then two, then ten, then eight, then one, then four. You only look at window number twelve if it rains or snows, because it is in the attic and you don't like it there. The dust up there feels heavy and hungry, and you're a little bit scared it will eat you up.

Today, it is cloudy, so you think you might have to go up there in a little bit. You know lots of things like this—clouds mean rain, but not always; open doors mean wind inside; smoke means be careful. Smoke has only happened a few times, and it's usually down the long dirt road, past where you think your body split open like a cocoon and made you.

You don't ever go past where you think your body split open like a cocoon and made you. You're not really sure, if you can even call her *your* body—she is the body that made you, which means *mother*, mostly, but you are not an infant; you were never an infant. And from books and faint memories, you're pretty sure that mothers don't fracture up like broken window glass and let you out. The house tells you that there were veiny cracks all over her skin when she made you, and that it was beautiful. The house says that your creation was perfect and important and vast, and you always preen a little bit at all those adjectives. You collect them and hold them so close to you until they become part of you too.

But that doesn't matter. What matters is, the smoke is usually past where you like to go, and the one time it wasn't is because the trees on the long dirt road got cut down and they spread the smoke too close to you. The house was a little bit hurt on the wall with window seven, but it was mostly fine because of the rain. It was stressful, but there were good things that came along with it. You got to see people, then—a small man with a smaller boy. They didn't see you, because nobody sees you. The small boy said, "Do you think the ghosts are still there?" and you had felt embarrassed, especially as the small man said, "Maybe the ghosts put out the fire," with a soft and knowing grin. You didn't do anything of the sort, so his kindness and his knowing were misplaced, which always feels *awful* to think about. You've let him down!

You imagine talking to the small man and apologizing, and he says, oh, it's okay! But you know he is just trying to make you feel better about your failures. You and the small man talk and talk and talk in your head until he tells you that you are bad and wrong and that you need to protect the house better. He scolds you in a way that makes him feel less small; it makes *you* feel small instead. You hate smallness on you because it squeezes and it aches. You wonder how the small man tolerates it, and you wonder even more how the smaller boy can even manage to survive it. You are always telling yourself stories like this about them.

You wish that you had done something brave, that you could do something brave, but you are, unfortunately, not terribly brave. The house assures you that this is fine when you're alone and quiet, but you don't really believe it. The house whispers a lot of things, and many of them are just trying to quell any concerns of yours. Its voice is old and breathy, and it wheezes in the cold. You wish you could care for it better, that you could wrap it up in yourself and keep it safe.

The rain starts soon after you think it might start, so you wander up to the attic and feel the dust there try to kiss you. You let it and you feel so flustered by the touch. Window number twelve is fine, but it needs to be closed tighter. This takes a considerable amount of strength, and you are not considerably strong by any means.

The rain stops around the same time you get the window shut, and then there is nothing for a little while. You don't like nothing; it makes you feel guilty, but at least feeling guilty usually moves you to do *something*. Today, that something is going outside to the long dirt road. The place where you think your body split open is not easy to spot, because she went into the dirt after that, but you know exactly where she was. It's not a very nice spot—it has a big, rugged rock that the small man and smaller boy used to trip over—but it's still her spot, so that means it's important, that means it's sacred. The house told you what sacred was not long after the two of you met. You let the moment take you. It isn't nothing if it's sacred, you know.

The after-rain of the dirt is so nice, so pleasant. You love it, you would hold it if you could. You would shape it in your hands and make it yours.

And so, you shape it in your hands and make it yours.

This is not how your story is supposed to go. You are weak and cowardly and big. But it goes like this anyways, with your hands suddenly *yours* again and your body, still cracked at every seam, builds around you in the mud. You run—you can't remember *running*—back to the house, as fast as you can, and you feel every single breath go in and out and in and out. Your stomach twists, like the big crawling vines in the green are choking it, and as you cross the threshold to inside, you keel over and cough brown, viscous blood onto the floorboards. It hurts, like tiny pebbles climbing up your neck. Everything is smaller, now, especially you.

You say, "House?" and nothing answers you, and everything is so empty that it aches. You can't say you've ached before, but you can say that it's unpleasant and no word fits cleanly like it. There are too many words that fit only for small things, and you hate it. Minutes away from it, you miss the comfort of being unsolid; you miss the day being the same.

The house is still silent, and the hands on this hideous *thing* you've been given are buzzing with nerves. You stay kneebound, begging to collapse in full. "Syncope" in the dictionary for mind and body disconnected, you remember, and you swallow the noun in prayer before another long cough. Less blood now, just iron-smelling fluids that are nowhere near as red. You haven't seen those in the dictionary, certainly.

Syncope takes you not long after, and it holds you tight until morning. You want it to keep you forever, but it seems you are less-than-lucky. The legs are faun-shaky, but you push this body up anyway, and it stands so tall that its stomach ties up a little bit. The house doesn't have water because it doesn't need it, but the body feels *dirty,* and why wouldn't it? It's wrong in every way, and it's trying to be you. You're not supposed to be anything. The house has whispered that you used to be a body, but you aren't anymore. You punch the wall and stumble for it; you try and say a word and only the wind comes out.

The biggest and least-broken mirror in the house is in the same room as windows seven and eight, where the walls peel with illustrated pink flowers. The only part wrong with the mirror is its top, which melted a bit in the fire. The body coughs at the dust and you hate its wrongness even more, but at least you can look at it. It's tall and shaky and bare, with dry-blood cracks going up everything. The hair from the head is long and dry with knots in it. Everything about this body is tied up! Stomach and hair and potential energy! You hate it more than you've ever hated anything at all.

There are paths to take. The house won't talk to you, so you need somebody else. You consider the small man or the boy, but they won't take well to a naked stranger with no clear words, you know from books. Still, you drape yourself in an old, old blanket and venture outside. It's still very much after-rain—the earth you just crawled from is muddy, and the treeleaves drip cold, clean water onto you—and you hate to call it yourself, but there's no easier way to think of it. That's your head, which came from the dirt and swallowed you yesterday. Now it has drops of water on it, coagulated so neatly onto the strands of hair that fall into your face, which is long and sharp.

It's the longest walk you can remember, and you hate it. Rocks pierce under your feet, and you feel your face move in on itself whenever they hurt. But you find the house, and you stare at it for a few long minutes. There is a small path of big rocks, all of them like the one that marked your sacred spot but flatter, that starts a little ways out, and you hop from stone to stone in case that's important.

You knock because you know very well about knocking. The small man's door was painted bright blue, once, but now it's not bright from time. Brown, woody veins peek through the chipping paint, and you stare at them for a long while until the hinges yell that the door is open. The small man is there, dressed in an old red shirt that says BENCHMARK I.T. SOLUTIONS FOURTH ANNUAL FUN RUN 2011 on it in fat, round letters.

"Hello," he says, with his brow moved all the way towards his nose, "Can I, um, help you?" He barely even grants that last part the dignity of a question mark.

"I'm from the house," you try to say, but all that comes out is a croak. You frown, and you sigh. You try to mime it instead, but you don't know how a body this unencompassing can show all of that. The small man purses his thin, chapped lips.

"How about tea."

You nod okay, even if you're not sure how tea will feel. He gestures, and you follow him inside, and he disappears for a moment, bringing back a big fluffy robe. He winces as you struggle to put it on, your arms getting the motions wrong a few times in a row. He proceeds to put a kettle on the stove, and he does not look at you at all until the kettle starts screaming. Soon, you have a cup (it is yellow and it says CONGRATULATIONS ON THE DIVORCE on it) with hot water and a small parcel at the bottom. You sip it and it tastes like nothing other than making your tongue hurt.

"Let's try talking again," the small man says. "Do you speak English?"

You nod, and then you croak again. You pull the robe tighter around your shoulders and he winces again. You try one last time, and say, "House," and you're proud of yourself for getting that one out.

"Your name is House?"

You cough, which stings, "I'm from it."

"This house?"

"The house. Not—so." You point down. "You said I put out a fire?"

"What?"

"The house. Down there. With the ghosts. That's. I'm—"

His lips go even thinner, to the point where they're flat and his dimpled cheeks puff out. He breathes out strangely, a few sharp times in a row. "Is this—what? Did Danny put you up to this?"

And you explain again, and he keeps breathing out at you until he shakes his head back and forth a few times. You tell him that the house won't talk to you and he squawks like a bird at that one. You start to frown at him, and you stand up and leave.

You walk back to the house in a huff, and when you walk in, it's still quiet. You drive your sharp knuckles into the sixth window about it, and you get even angrier when it stings.

The next few days, you sleep. You think you sleep, at least. You don't dream at all, and the house doesn't tell you anything, so you just stay curled up on the motheaten bed and you don't move other than the occasional toss and turn. The silence bites at you but you ignore it, other than praying that the scabs on your hand break and bleed more on the sheets. Your stomach sings to you, and you hate the sound. You had always hoped that bodies were good to have, that you had enjoyed whatever you had before this, but now, you know that it is entirely misery. On the rare occasion that you open your eyes, the sight of everything hurts and hurts and hurts.

The house would tell you how to get better. Its silence proves, you decide, that you will never get better at all. You have ruined your story and stomped all over the chance to be good and it's all because you got too caught up in yourself.

You breathe deep and harsh into the holes in the fabric, into the springs that poke your too-tender skin. You hear noises from you and you only—drumming in your chest like a hailstorm, buzzing in your head like nothing at all. You feel rage, which fizzes out into apathy, which fizzes out into something beyond apathy. It's flatness, it's empty, it's *small*. You take the empty and the smallness and you hold them tight. They're yours, more than the house or the body or anything. Your dry mouth, skin peeling off its lips, smiles at the thought.

Hunger and thirst try and fail to wake you for what seems like ages. You call their bluffs, dig yourself deeper into the crevices of the mattress until you can pretend you're dead. It doesn't feel familiar, which you think it should—you've been buried for so long but you can't even know the feeling? It's infuriating—but again, the fury works its way to soft, sweet blankness. You could fall in love with blankness, even beyond the gentle intimacy you find with it already.

There are noises in the house, eventually. Not from the house itself, but from others. Footsteps, tapping loudly, and, as you notice them, the door slamming. And two voices, familiar—the small boy, followed soon after by the small man. They're here, and you start to shake for it. They gossip about you. The small man laughs at you and the boy says, *this is ridiculous*, and you want to cry massive tears from your new-old eyes until the room they're in floods and drowns them.

You don't actually want that. Wanting that would make you the worst person ever, and you're barely even a person, so you have to be very careful about goodness.

Eventually, they find you. The boy has big, round eyes, and when he looks at you, they get rounder. He's holding a flashlight, which hurts your already-hurting eyes. The man jumps at the sight of you. He's holding a steak knife and he nearly drops it, but he steadies his grip. He's wearing a different shirt, one without any words on it. You croak again as you try to greet him.

He says something, voice quivering, but you can't make out the words. You're distracted by looking down at yourself—the ribs draped clearly in thin skin, the crawling rot on your healing hand. You stare at the man, and he stares back, and you want the floor to swallow him, so it does.

You don't mean for it to happen, but the wooden floor cracks wide open and the man falls through, and the boy screams loudloudloud as he drops his flashlight. You see the man, writhing in pain over the base of the house, and you can't stand to look at him. So the ceiling crumbles to bury him, slow at first until you exhale. The boy is weeping now, and you're weeping too. The whole house weeps with you. The boy's big eyes well with water, and you shake your head at him until he runs far, far away. You hear a noise of pain from under the rubble that you and the house have caused. You hear the noises for hours and hours, and each time you shudder, another window breaks.

He dies early in the morning, with the sun just barely teasing its arrival, and you hear the softest shatter from the twelfth window, two floors up.

He never even bothers to join you.

A Tendency To Devour

SHE WOKE UP THAT morning mud-covered and brackish. She'd slept in the pond all night hoping it would make something whole out of her, but all it had done was make her feel nauseous. She vomited—mostly dirt, with blood to accompany it.

The people who had slept here before her were beautiful people, gently preserved by wet, maternal peat. She dreamt of them every night, and she saw them floating near her now. Three women, perfectly still. Still beautiful, still sated.

She wished, more than anything, to be sated. Her brother had always given her sharp looks for too much on her plate, even if there was enough to spare. She was hungry, and no one ever liked her for that.

Slowly, unsurely, she pulled herself up to stand. Her joints all cracked like smooth, smooth stones crashing against each other in a harsh current; she was too quick to be at home in the stillness, no matter how much she wanted it. Her skin was cold, growing colder by the second, but she couldn't bring herself to care much about that at all given the hopelessness of the situation. She was *starving*; she was desperate for something, for anything.

The trees, bold as ever in their midwinter nudeness, waved their branches hello, and she did not wave back. Instead, she fell to her knees and begged to be loved.

⋯◆⋯

The first body had shown up when she was right on the cusp of adolescence, which was a predictably dreadful sort of time. Her brother took her out to see it when their father was away on Official Business. Her brother said that he might as well. He had said several other things, most of which she forgot about very quickly. That night, her brother drank beer that made his fifteen-year-old mouth twist with revulsion that he tried to hide from his friends, and she, friendless on account of her shyness and strange demeanor, stared wide-eyed at the woman in the water.

The woman was middle-aged, taller than average, and round-faced. Her long hair which fanned out loose behind her like a crane wing was dark brown and curled tightly. Her hands were calloused, and her hips were small. No one had seen her before, though very few people were asked about knowing her in the first place. A particularly rakish man from town seemed more frightened than everybody else, so maybe he was a liar and knew her properly. Or maybe he was scared. The girl didn't know, and never cared to find out. If he knew her, he didn't love her, and his revulsion towards her floating body only further proved his lack of decency.

Despite the teenagers yelling, the body was sound asleep, her arms laying softly across her stomach—covered, like most of her body, in soft green something. The girl couldn't stop herself—she touched the woman's forehead, fingers spread wide, palm slightly cupped. The cold smoothness of it felt better, softer than anything the girl had felt before. She continued to prod at the woman's form, eventually pulling at the green that grew all over it. With a child's curiosity, she smelled it—sweet, but earthy—and subsequently placed it in her mouth. When she tasted that vegetal softness, she felt like she was a miracle, too. She swallowed it down quickly and nearly choked.

She could be enchanted like this woman was, and she would be safe and watched by everyone. They would talk about her, they would whisper about her, they would want to know every last detail about her. They would burn pyres in her honor and love her while she laid perfectly still and got eaten up by that green, green magic.

Her brother took her home that night earlier than either of them would have preferred to leave. He had struck up a conversation with his pretty friend from school who let him copy their answers; the smoke from the bonfires caused the girl to have a coughing fit. Something brown and almost-bloody that accompanied the coughs stained her nice yellow dress, the one her father called Sunday Best even as their family did nothing of note on Sundays. She was draped over her brother's bony shoulder, coughing out tiny storms onto the stone path. He'd made her honey-in-tea and he'd drawn her a bubble bath, all while chastising her for ruining his chance to do something important with that pretty classmate. In the bathwater, she pretended to be the body; shaped the soap over her body as a substitute for sweet algae.

It wasn't the same—nothing could be the same. The water was too hot, and the soap too uncoagulated to make the pretending feel worth it, in the end.

⸺◦⸺

The second body came a year or two after that. A young woman, this time familiar to most in town. Her warm skin had been tinted ashy, but she was otherwise the same as she'd always been—delicate, pretty, kindhearted. This was the type of woman people talked about fondly, but with tones far too wolflike for comfort. Her long neck and her round breasts were the subject of whispers that she never heard, or, at least, that she didn't seem to have heard. She seemed happier than those sorts of whispers usually left girls like her. Even sleeping-dead, she looked serene, she looked blissful.

The body had been fine the day prior, helping her mother paint kitchen walls. The mother had said, *she had wanted to go for a walk last night,* and then—the mother sobbed, and she screamed, a wretched, painful sound that made birds fly away. She put her face in her hands and started clawing at it, pulling at her hair and pushing at her eye sockets until someone stopped her. The scratches left thick, red swollen lines up her face, and her eyes bulged more than they had before. The mother's hands twitched as she was held back, wanting to do *more.* The young girl, watching the scene, understood. She considered painting red lines up her face, because her nails were cut too short to claw productively.

Unlike with the first body, which floated several meters away from this one, the girl was frightened to the point of near disgust of going near the second. The first body was a stranger, something foreign and explorable, but this body was something she could touch and then she'd *know* that she'd ruined it; how she ruined it. (She ruined many things, her father told her on his worst nights.) Still, the fear twisted itself into *need,* as many feelings did for her, and eventually, she couldn't help herself—the moon and stars begged her to visit. Begged her to brush the woman's dark, silken hair out of her face, to feel its coldness, to feel *desire.*

Minnows swam around the girl's ankles, nibbling them, eventually biting them bloody and raw, teeth far longer and sharper than they had ought to be. Sharp stones dug into her, cut her, fell into the wounds left by the fish, dirtied them and made them sick. Even so, she couldn't bring herself to move away from the body, so peaceful and beautiful in the moonlight that it made the girl's chest burn. She touched the neck, felt it give—her hand flew back to her side with a strange snap, gripping something sturdy and metal-smelling that she couldn't let go of. She couldn't look at it, either, not until she had run home, her fishbloody steps staining the hardwood floor.

Her father and brother were asleep, thankfully. With her free hand, she fetched a bucket of water, and then a rag after that, and she sat herself where the blood began to seep into the woodgrains like tiny rivers.

Her other hand—even bloodier than the floor—held a small, flattish bone: a circle with a hollow crown shape on top of it. She examined it closely—its imperfect lumps, its browning redness, and imagined it was hers. This was a body that was wanted; this was a body that could never ruin anything. The girl stared at the bone for as long as she could stare without her eyes going dry, and then she stared at it a few moments more. She needed to keep this safe, she knew, and she knew it even more the longer she looked at it. She needed it to stay with her, and to become her.

She opened her mouth to exhale, and she swallowed the bone whole. It was painless, save for some scratching in her throat, but that went away quickly, with just the feeling of an almost-wound to savor. She shut her eyes, and savored the moment—the barely-open window sending night breezes onto her heavy back, the smell of soap, the taste of marrow.

The floors were not too much work to clean, and the fish bites were easy enough to cover with heavy socks and a demand for privacy. She felt a rush in her own blamelessness, a joy in her escape. The slight off-color of the floors or the scars on her feet were not the sort of things her father noticed. And her brother, he noticed, but he said nothing, just looked at her with sad, sad eyes.

No one commented on the cavity in the second body's neck—it's perfectly reasonable that some creature, perhaps a vulture, perhaps a cat, took the opportunity to try a new sort of delicacy. The body's mother, always red-eyed and wont to keeping her doors locked, never even noticed it at all.

Years passed before the third body showed itself. Her brother was off in the city, working for some family their father knew well, and her father hardly cared about what she did so long as it didn't stain his name more than either of them already had. The townspeople were whispering about the body the moment it surfaced—an out-of-towner, a woman—the girl's age—who sold bread at the farmer's market. Her long, black hair flowed out around her in the pondwater, so beautiful that it seemed like she had been destined to sleep in this water, and one of her dark, dark eyes was wide open, unblinking and unseeing.

The girl—a woman now, though most still thought her to be a girl on account of her constant worry, her self-imposed smallness—found herself taken with the body, even more so than the two that preceded it. She'd seen it before, selling bread and pastries, and she'd been taken with it then too, touching its hand for a second too long and whispering a *thank you* before running home with her face boiling hot. Now, however, it was *enthralling*. The gossiping crowds subsided by evening, that first day, and the teenagers were far too busy with their own affairs to care as much as the teenagers of years before did. But she stayed. She couldn't help but stay. She stayed alone and silent, standing sentinel, standing vigil.

She remembered the rightness of that bone in her mouth. She had not felt whole since then. She had tried to feel whole in as many ways as she could. Her own blood, her own muscle, her own bone disgusted her, but still, she tried to feel whole with them. Companionship, too, felt empty—tongues, teeth, and come did little besides make her feel hungrier. She worked odd jobs, made enough money to keep herself afloat, but that was just floating. She wanted far more than that, and want, for her, became the usual *need*.

Returning to the first two bodies felt *wrong*, as she had already taken so much from them. She had almost taken more bones from the second one, only to find that something had rooted in the neck cavity, tiny wildflowers crawling onto the pretty sleeping face. To ruin that body any more would be criminal.

This is to say, a new body was a blessing. The girl felt so terribly empty, so terribly needy, and this would be her salvation. She was sure of it. The body's smooth skin, its glassy eyes, were perfect.

She stared with the sweet, vegetal algae, which she feasted upon eagerly, her sharp teeth tearing into it like candyfloss. The sudden nudeness of the third body shocked her, just a bit, but it interested her too—she wondered how the flesh would give in, if the greenness of the algae shell had seeped into the blood, if the heart under the soft curve of its left breast would give the slightest twitch. That thought quickly consumed her, and she swiped her nails, now sharp with age and patience, across the body's sternum. She felt a cold hand on her own, saw the body staring one-eyed and hungry right at her. "Please," the body said, voice waterlogged but wanting.

So, the girl dug deeper into the sternum, and then, moved over to the breast. Seeing the heart intact, she smiled warmly, and, like a lover, began to tongue at it. The body, slowly, began to grab back at her—to place a cold, cold hand on her thigh, to squeeze at her. Strange, drowning groans filled the grove around them.

The heart was strange, salty in taste. Like meat, but thicker. The girl couldn't bring herself to bite into something so beautiful, so she simply toyed with it, until she felt it move once, then twice, 'til the body grabbed her by the waist and pulled her underwater.

"You're beautiful," the body said, voice clear, "Thank you for visiting me."

The girl's eyes stung, unused to the water, but she kept them open, tried to lean in to kiss the body, which smiled sadly at her.

"Not yet, hungry girl," the body cooed. The body's own blood, flowing beautifully from her chest, surrounded her like fog in the water. "Not yet."

In her following visits, the body never spoke to her. Sometimes, she swore that the open eye followed her as she walked through the grove, but she only swore it to herself. She had no one else to swear it to. She wanted, with a certain determination that she could not even dream to describe, to speak to the body again, to bring life back into that heart with her hunger and her need.

So, she made a plan. And on a crisp, winter evening, she took her coat off by the rocks, laid it out flat, and she went to sleep in the pond. She hadn't dreamt at all, save for the brief thought of fishbones covered in mud.

When she woke, she begged and begged and begged to nothing at all. She imagined a lover's touch, but all she received was absence and cruel rejection.

She wrapped herself in her coat out of eventual necessity, and imagined it was green, that it was candyfloss. She imagined floating in that pond, full and beloved. But that was impractical, she sighed. She heard *not yet, hungry girl* fly around in her mind, and wanted to scream about it, but couldn't bring herself to make the noise.

Instead, she bit her own lip and began to walk home, sickened by the blood her teeth drew.

Litany For The Un-selfed

Somewhere different, where the world is stranger and the fog crawls up people's ankles to give their steps purpose, there are ways to become. It's arcane knowledge, and becoming is never a pleasant thing to partake in, but for some, it is horribly necessary. Who hasn't heard tales of those beasts from somewhere *else* different tricking ingénues and adventurers alike into giving up their names and lives? Who hasn't reached out for something new?

These sorts of ceremonies are long and complicated and arduous, but you already know this. There are rules to follow, and steps to this ceremony that you need so desperately. Morning and evening, you cry, but with your eyes uncovered and unweeping, there is a path for you. It is made of what follows:

1. **Bird blood and entrails.**

2. **Intestines line the ground like pink wire; they form an almost perfect circle.**

3. **The wax from a candle hits the ground in tiny drops.**

The flame is strong, but the black of the wick is clear inside of it. Your hand twitches as the wax meets it, but you let it stain your hands first-degree. It will make them clean.

4. Bones, foraged from the woods.

5. The plants and fungi that grow near them. You stare at them, swallow them, drink them as tea and hope to see something. Sometimes you do.

6. The remains of your name, which you have not borne in years.

I am made for storytelling, and I am not made for speaking about myself. I am nameless, faceless, and I accept this about my being, but I would not inflict it on you. The pronoun *I* terrifies me. There is intimacy that I have not earned, there is violation in getting too close to the subject. I am breaking rules for you. I am telling this story because you need a story told. Can you hear me? Can you follow my words?

1. Salt so coarse it hurts your tongue. Your mother told you that your taste for salt was the only reason she could know you weren't some sort of changeling. You tried very hard to dislike salt from then on.

2. Your first vision is one of the forest, which is made of the long-dead, the blighted, and the bodies that are like yours. This place is nothing but rot-to-be, but you want the potential of more from it. You want it to grow roots, you want it to rise up as trees.

3. A second candle, lit with a match. The wax drips less, but it still burns.

4. When they took your name, you felt the weight of it

float out of your veins, and you saw the branches on the ground around you go as red as arteries.

5. Yew needles and dust.

6. The stories your mother told you to make you scared of the dark.

7. One of them went like this: Back in the village all the stories are written in, two sisters lived together in a little wooden house. The house was shoddy and its walls were covered in chipping paint. The older sister, handsome and wise, warned her sister of the folk who lived in the woods; she warned her of their lies, their fruits, their teeth. She said, do not even look at them; she said, they will take everything there is to take from you. And the younger sister, pretty and curious, listened, of course, as anyone should listen to their elders. But her curiosity nipped at her until it possessed her, and one night, as the older sister slept, the younger sister snuck out to the woods.

8. A lock of your hair.

9. The blade you used to cut it.

10. When the younger sister entered the woods, she felt her heart leap through her chest until it was near-bursting. Everything around her was so bright, so beautiful; she hadn't even known that so many colors existed in the world. Each fruit, each flower, each speck of lichen that ate the logs—all of it was new and wonderful and enthralling. The folk who dwelled in the woods spoke sweet words to her. There were verses laced with sugar, touches full of wanting, wine aged for eternities. The younger sister feasted and kissed and sang, and the

sharp teeth of the forest folk glistened like crystals in the seeping-through starlight.

How did the folk who live in the woods speak so sweetly to her? Was it nice to be dined and loved by them? Why did curiosity possess her? Where did her sister hear of the folk who live in the woods? Curiosity is a hungry necessity. I cannot tell a story like this one, but this is the story you were told.

1. **A prayer that you mumble instead of memorizing.**

2. **Another match, as the candle flickers out. You curse at the air, but this is the nature of things.**

3. **The younger sister woke in the shoddy wooden house, nameless and sickly. The older sister found her and wept over pale skin and a knifesharp ribcage. So frail and overindulged, the un-selfed younger sister promised, voice weak, that she would stay with the older sister forever. Curiosity had possessed her, and it seemed that now, it might kill her. She died in her sister's arms that night and her grave said nothing at all.**

4. **The hand skin that peels off with the wax that's started to grate at you.**

5. **The pinprick of blood that follows the skin.**

6. **The crack of your wrist. The sound reverberates all around you, and you remember to spread more entrails, to make another circle.**

7. **Your second vision is one of your mother. Her face is stern and her stomach and throat are tight with worry and full of stories. She gave you her eyes and**

her skeleton, but she was not particularly satisfied with how you used them. Now, she asks for them back. You say no, no, I can't give you anything else, and she calls you ungrateful, tells you that your breath reeks of berries. She calls you changeling again, and you want to tell her she's right, but that would be a lie. You are her flesh, her blood, her bone, and both of you will have to learn to live with that.

My mother told stories, too. She told them smoothly and easily; they went down like molasses. She never told me that my stories were wrong, only different—but her stories were the ones I wanted to tell for a long time. I don't like confessing these sorts of things. You are no changeling, and I am no mother, and we are all ourselves, even as yourself has been taken from you.

Your elbows are too sharp. As you set up this ceremony, you throw them toward me by accident, no control of your spindlelimbs. I will not admit that I am charmed by this out loud, but I will admit it here, and I will watch as you eat the bittersour fruit you weren't supposed to eat.

1. **A wince.**

2. **A spit-out seed.**

3. **Your curiosity.**

4. **It wasn't curiosity that took you to the woods, so much as it was rebellion. And it was hardly rebellion. More than anything, it was just something to do. You couldn't sleep at night, and you had already counted the planks of wood on the floor, already sorted the rocks you'd collected from the pond near the markets, already considered waking your mother. You wanted something *new*.**

5. **Tidied-up intestines. Your circles have grown sloppy.**

6. **The forest was not quite like the stories your mother told you. The colors were ones you knew well, ones you'd seen plenty of times before. They were still lovely and you wished you were the type of person who could paint, instead of the type of person who tried to see visions, so that you could capture the beauty of it. It was no bacchanal, no frenzy of sublimity, it was just the woods, beautiful and kind. The folk who live in the forest were beautiful, but hardly any more beautiful than anyone else. They offered you fruits and gentle touches and songs, which you took, but their teeth were not much sharper than yours, and they did not leave you to wake up half-dead and without a soul. Their fruits were sweet, with just the right amount of tartness as they broke open in your mouth.**

I tell stories. That is what I am. I write, I speak, I dream. I know stories like this, like yours, and they end too cruel for me to stomach. It's not that I dislike cruelty—it's often necessary to push forward that which needs to be pushed forward—but rather that I want a fairer sort of tale. An ethical unselfing, a kinder submission to the unknown.

1. **The tightness of your shoulders, the length of your spine.**

There is no story to tell about me. There are many stories to tell about you. I want to tell them all. I want a tome tucked in each of your ribs, I want printing-press letters on all your vertebrae. Every morning, a new set of words all around you.

I am a selfish narrator, maybe. You are unselfed without a name, but you are gone entirely without stories. I want to raise you from the dead for as long as I can.

1. Another sip, another swallow.

2. Your third vision is one of the birds, cut open and gutted. You feel their pain, you feel your own guts falling out of you, but you did what you needed to do to see something, to see anything. You are the birds, the rot, the bodies, and you are the remains of your name.

3. An exhale.

4. An inhale.

5. They took your name when they found you the next morning, wide-eyed and half-drunk. Your mother looked ashamed that you had fallen for such tricks, and she helped them rip your name out of you piece by miserable piece. You felt lighter. You felt ill. You returned to the woods.

6. An exhale.

7. Burnt fingers from a snuffed-out candle, as you stand up and prepare yourself for a grand return.

I will follow you there, and everywhere after.

HOT SINGLES IN YOUR AREA!

THE BANNER AD SAYS I'M LONELY...WANNA CHAT? in hot pink letters that make Julia want to rip her eyeballs out of her head, and then under that, there's a slightly fried JPEG of River Seely-Burke from back in high school, who killed herself four years after graduation. Julia's grandmother had been obsessive about the whole ordeal; she printed out each slide from a presentation that Julia and River had made for tenth-grade English class, laminated them, and left them at River Seely-Burke's gravesite.

River Seely-Burke's tits are falling out of her too-small tank top. She looks mostly like she did in all the memorial posts and on the funeral program in Julia's car's glove compartment—same deer wide-eyes, same hair that was too intentionally messy to not be salon-cut. Her expression is a bit more intense than Julia remembers her ever looking, but, well, people change, so maybe she got more solemn before she killed herself. That maybe tends to happen. Except that in some pamphlets, Julia's read that suicidal people seem happier right before they kill themselves. Julia has never become happier in all her years of passive suicidality, but she's also never killed herself, so perhaps she wouldn't be able to judge?

Distracted from the shitty ancient webcomic that her friend had sent her, Julia screenshots the ad, hovers over it to find a shortened URL, and sighs as she clicks it to at least get the information. It's a predictably uncreative site, from its address (*photo takedown* and *bot* and *crypto mining* autofill when she searches it) to its design; there are columns and columns of pixelated women, name and age and sign in the top right corner. This design choice obscures some of the faces, but River's is in plain sight—RIVER, 21, VIRGO. It's accurate information, too. River and Julia were hardly *friends*, but she'd always brought cupcakes from that expensive vegan bakery in the city to school on her birthday, which was always just a few days after school started. And she'd been a year younger than Julia, who was in possession of an October birthday just past the commonwealth's grade cutoff, and Julia was, three years after River's passing, twenty-five years old.

This sort of site doesn't seem the type of place that River would put herself on. She didn't seem the type to go into sex work at all, but if she did, it would be on some sort of spiritual-wellness angle; she would be camming surrounded by chunky crystals and herbal concoctions. And even if this *was* something River had done on her own volition—God knows, Julia didn't talk to her at all towards the end, she could've changed dramatically—it still felt ethically kind of vomit-inducing to use a dead girl's image to shill for a poorly designed cybersex service. But Julia was never really one to partake in any of this sort of thing–it felt like she was doing something deviant, not knowing if the people she derived pleasure from wanted her to derive that pleasure. Partners have laughed at her for it, which, she supposes, is far.

Julia messages the chat—first ten messages free!—after a failed attempt at figuring out how takedown requests work in this sort of situation.

user12108: Please take down this profile; the woman featured passed away several years ago.

River's face is looking right at her, unblinking. She's pretty, really, she always was. There are moments in staring at the bouncing ellipses where it almost seems like she's moving, breathing, blinking. Julia hasn't slept enough lately, really. A response pops up, and then another one, and then another one.

River: hiiiiii
River: promise you im real LOL i can send pics
River: whats yr name?

Julia looks at that for a solid minute until an image file is sent—another photo of River, waist up, wearing only an ill-fitting bra and jewelry. It's still recognizably *her*, but it's overexposed, and her makeup is too heavy, too dark around the eyes to be true to her spirit. There is a hickey on her left breast, just barely visible beneath the bra, and there is a pout on her face. She looks desirable, Julia thinks, she looks whole. Or, no. This River looks tired. She looks haggard and alone. But she looks—

River: wanna see more?
user12108: River passed away three years ago.
River: LOLLLL yr so so funny! im super alive and my skin is so so soft. fr tho whats yr name?

Julia winces and apologizes to her cousin in her head.

user12108: Helena. this is really disrespectful and I am going to send this page to the dead girl's family.

Despite herself, Julia can't help but want to chase this conversation further and further. She wants to ask questions and not be afraid. She wonders, did River say these words while she was alive? Would River know her name? Was River's skin soft as it looked in this photograph, and would she let someone like Julia even come close to it?

Julia unclenches her jaw, and notices a pain in her lip; her teeth have been caught on it, and now, there is a faint taste of bit skin. But no matter—two more messages.

River: i am alive and softskin and flesh. do u want to see more?

River: we dont have to lie to each other bbygirl Tell me your real name i will be so nice and pretty with it <3 i bet it's super cute !

user12108: please do not send any more images. You are beautiful but this is wrong

Another image is linked, but Julia doesn't click it. Her hands and eyes feel heavy and loud under her skin, and there is too salty sweat hanging from her brow. Her stomach rumbles and warms at once. She does not click the link.

River: i thought u wanted proof LOL. i live here and i have a body and i am so there and so heavy in it! my blood pumps so hard. i bet you know a lot about blood pumping hard considering you're on here ;)

user12108: My blood is unremarkable

YOU HAVE USED HALF OF YOUR FREE MESSAGES! LOG IN AND SUBSCRIBE TO OUR PREMIUM SERVICE (USD \$2.99/month) TO GET DEEPER! OTHER PAYMENT PLANS AVAILABLE*

Julia clicks the photo link, and the bile that had already been creeping toward her tongue is suddenly all she can taste.

At first, it's just the nudity. Julia has seen her share of naked bodies, but the sight of River's bare breasts, the curve of her shoulders, makes Julia feel *evil*. She has violated this poor corpse's history. Except, she received it, and the River-thing wanted her to see it, so—no, there is more to see and say.

Then, there is the state of the photo itself. Once again, the photo seems overexposed, or maybe like it's been edited to be low-contrast; it's a very early-10s sort of aesthetic choice, if it's an aesthetic choice at all. Except, exposure and contrast wouldn't make sense given the eyes—glassy and ink-black—or the hair—lighter than Julia remembers, sure, but still a natural color. It's just her skin that's off.

And that's when Julia starts to notice the details of the body; certain joints are bloated strangely, the hickey on River's chest is too long, too deep, too wine-colored to be a hickey. The mark has a slight serration to it, and there are reddish-bluish striations peeking out of it. Julia imagines the mark if it were on her own chest, presses down on where it would be until she can feel her pulse shake her whole body. Her own skin is rougher than it should be, goosebumped and burdened with bone beneath it.

user12108: My name is Julia.

River: such a cute name omg…i wish you would show me your skin i bet its also so cute.

user12108: It is not. where are you right now? You should be buried.

River: you need to learn self love julia <3 your skin is cute and yours just like mine is so strong and of-me. Your skin could be mine too. i could treat it so nice ;) Can u put webcam on? I will join

And Julia complies. She peels the tape off her laptop's camera. She's not sure why. She wants proof of River's reality, maybe, or she wants to impress River. Maybe it is an exchange—an observation for an observation, a breast for a breast.

Glassy-eyed and pixelated, River appears, still naked, in a rectangle above the one that shows Julia. "Hello," says River's voice, but it chops in the middle. "You can't use your microphone unless you go deeper. You can say three more things to me with your keyboard first." Her voice is stilted, as are her movements, even as the quality of the video and sound improve. She tilts her neck like each degree of movement is a delicate moment of puppetry, she holds her hand over the cut on her chest and, rhythmically, jerks every ten seconds or so. Her hair is tousled perfectly, wisps in all the right places even as her face looks so sunken. "Before you type anything else, Julia," and she says Julia's name like it means something, "Can you show me your skin?"

Julia obliges, despite the shame that pools around her for it. River makes a noise that sounds pleased, and Julia works faster, until she has ripped every layer off her body, until she is bare and ready for River to see her.

user12108: am I good enough?

River says, "You are everything we need. You can become so much. Your skin is yours and mine, isn't it? Feel it, and let it grow soft with my touch. Okay?"

Julia touches her own skin and she lets herself pretend it is River's hand touching it, allowing herself to flinch from the shock of its coldness. River calls her "Good," or maybe Julia calls herself good, as her skin smoothes over, as it becomes of-her and of-River and heavy and alive. River says, "You need to give me something, alright? Alternative payment plan. It's super easy, and it," she hums dreamily, and a little less-than-three pops up in the chatbox. "You know?"

The hand scratches down Julia's neck until it settles on her left breast, and then she types:

user12108: I have a pocketknife

River says, her pouting mouth beautiful and half-breathing, "Take it in our hand." So she does. And River's hand has a steadier grip than Julia's ever did. How many dead girls have held this knife with her before? Who held the knife that cut River open? She considers asking, but she only has one message left. So:

user12108: I'll be with you?

"And so many others. It's nice in here. People will talk to you and want you. I... it's a new life. And it's a perfect one. I don't remember much of what happened before my skin was mine and my blood pumped hard and cold, but I wasn't wanted then. I am so wanted now. You want me. Did you want me before?"

Julia shakes her head no and feels tears well up from the shame.

The hand she shares with River moves for her, carves a clean circle through soft skin and fat and tissue until her heart can shake her whole body as she looks at it, its veins and arteries pulsing like worms around the wound she and River built together. And she closes her eyes and she is whole, whole, whole.

Julia's skin is hers and it is soft and everyone wants to talk to her. Her heart beats hard and beautifully and she is never even lonely at all.

THERE IS A CREATURE LIVING AND GROWING INSIDE OF YOU

THE CALL COMES WHEN Jonah is on her second five-dollar IPA of the evening. Her chest tightens up at the caller ID, but she stands up and walks to the single area of this shitty microbrewery that isn't packed and she takes three deep breaths before pressing the little green icon. There are the standard formalities —is this you, this is Dr. Fuentetodos, et cetera. And then:

"Well, it's not toxic," which, all things considered, is good news, "Obviously, it isn't... harmless, considering your symptoms, and considering the fact that it is a Creature growing inside of your head, but we can rule out that particularly unfortunate scenario."

"That's," she says, and then she stops talking, and coughs out another dark, round seed. That's all she's been coughing out lately. She always means to plant them, but usually, she decides not to.

"I'm going to order more labs for you. Try and get them done in the next week or so—nine AM and fasting from midnight, nothing but water or black coffee" and he laughs for three seconds, "But you're used to this whole song and dance by now, aren't you?"

"Yes. I'm sorry about the background noise, I'm—"

"It's okay. Should I call you back tomorrow morning?" By tomorrow morning, he means tomorrow afternoon, and by I, he means the receptionist at his office reading off a sheet of paper.

"No, I can—I'd prefer to keep it all in one call," and she forces a smile, hoping that it comes through in her tone. She is polite. She is reacting in the proper way. She is normal. There is something green and sharp toothed and beautiful in the back of her throat, and she is normal, she is fine. "Should I—are there precautions I should take? New meds?"

"I would recommend reaching out to your psychiatrist about the doses of your anti-depressants if you haven't already."

"We upped the... um, bupropion to," the string lights above are making her dizzy, so it takes her a moment to recall, "Three hundred once per day."

"Great. I'm going to wait for these labs before we put you on anything new, okay? Take care of yourself, and I'll call you back once we have results. Feel free to call the office with any concerns, though."

Dr. Fuentetodos is young, barely out of residency. He has a close-shaved beard and wire-fred glasses. He wears novelty ties. He has read all the essays about women whose doctors tell them they're imagining things; he implies, unsubtly, that those doctors' failures bring him shame as a man. He says, it is a privilege to treat you and to help you understand this Creature that lives and grows inside of your head. He is different from the last neurologist, and the one before that.

He is still immensely frustrating. His sweet voice and his politeness don't make up for the bureaucracy or the money or the lack of answers. So Jonah ends the call simply with, "Okay, thanks," and nothing else. She downs the rest of her five-dollar IPA and walks up to the bar, closes her tab, leaves a two-dollar bill as a tip.

The metro stop is not too far, but it's far enough that Jonah grows dizzier the whole walk there, and she's seeing long dark shapes while she swipes her card and pushes through the turnstile. She squints, and they writhe like worms. They writhe and they writhe, and Jonah smiles, tilts her head to the left, watches the worms drip down and down and down. They could dig into her, she thinks, could enrich the body for her green, green friend so sweetly and kindly. She sees the worms split apart, but she doesn't worry—she knows her worm facts well, knows about their possession of five whole hearts. Her own dreadfully singular heart picks up its pace at the thought, accelerates to hummingbird-fast so it can compensate for her lacking.

"Sorry," a voice says, and she ricochets back to unwormliness, "Are you okay?"

It's a woman her father's age wearing a sweater too thick for the springtime. Her forehead is creased tight, her heavy eyelids droop low with an almost frustrating level of pity.

"I'm. Yes," Jonah eventually stutters out. "I found out that the Creature growing inside of my brain is not poisoning me."

"Well, that's worth celebrating," and the crease leaves, the eyes open slightly, "Happy for you, sweetpea. But you've been standing here for—"

"I'll go catch my train, yes."

"—ten, fifteen minutes. I thought you might be... on something, and well, my kid, they've got friends who," and then she holds up a nasal spray, "So they told me, Momma, you need to keep these on hand, and they're a smart kid—really gifted, really kind—and so I listen to them. But you're not on anything?"

"Just two light beers and medications as prescribed," Jonah says, noting how slow her speech starts, so she picks it up, "No, but, I'm fine—your kid is smart for that, yeah. I'm going to go get my train, thank you, okay, bye," and she darts off, a plan which is foiled by her train being eight minutes away and the woman being on the same line as her. She tries to engage, to be polite. "Do you get—um. Do you get sweaty. In the sweater."

"I get cold very easily," the woman shrugs, "It's better to have too many layers than too few."

"Yeah, that makes sense. Sorry that I asked."

"You're clearly having a strange day; I can forgive an awkward conversation starter." She holds out her hand, "Erica."

"Jonah. Thank you for checking in on me. I'm just… overwhelmed."

"Aren't we all? I mean, I don't have a Creature inside of my head, of course—and aren't I lucky for that!—but life is life even without one. Can't imagine how it is for you!" Erica offers a hug, which is ultimately not given.

The train comes a minute early, and Jonah coughs out another seed.

⸺◆⸺

Jonah had a seizure on her twenty-third birthday. She had never had one before, though she had always been worried about them after reading about them in a first aid guidebook as a child, a book that had a quarter of the pages tea-stained beyond legibility. She had no interest in medicine herself, but it was in her father's bedroom, so it felt very grown-up to read it. She didn't like picturing the brain as electric, and she couldn't get the cartoonish image of that wet organ being shocked by lightning bolts out of her head.

Jonah had a seizure on her twenty-third birthday. She was at her apartment, her friends were there, everyone was tipsy and wearing cowboy outfits; it was a good night. She remembers taking her first bite of cake (chocolate with strawberries), and then she remembers seeing green and feeling hungry. And then, she was in a hospital bed, being teased by a nurse for thrashing around so much in her sleep that the IV kept falling out. "You only have so many veins!" the nurse laughed, and then looked at Jonah with thin, dark eyes, "You've been up a few times, but you've been hazy. Your buddies brought you here, do you remember that?"

She shook her head, and the nurse nodded his, "That's okay, you've had a big day. You feel like you're gonna fall asleep again?" and she shook her head again, pushed herself up to sitting. "Alright, the doctor's gonna be here in a few minutes, but I gotta ask you some questions first, okay?"

It was a bland interview—information about her and her medical history—and a bland visit to the hospital. The most exciting part was the brain scan, the sting of the adhesives on her scalp, and the MRI that followed soon after. The thrum and click of the machine sounded like music, and it was stuck in her head for the hours she waited before the phrase "we're not really sure," came out of the doctor's mouth and she introduced Jonah to Dr. Aker, Neurology.

Dr. Aker was very convinced that Jonah was fine. She said, it can happen with low blood sugar, or a lack of electrolytes, or flashing lights. Dr. Aker said, it might just be a freak accident. And Jonah was perfectly okay with that.

Or, Jonah was perfectly okay with it until the next day, back in her own bedroom, she saw bruise-colored lines crawling down from the back of her neck, and she coughed out a soft pink petal.

◆

The Creature that lives and grows inside of Jonah's head is beautiful and strong. It has tendrils that feel like silk and honeysweet petals that look like the morning sky. Sometimes, Jonah thinks that she is better off with it than without it, because, historically, she has not had that sort of luck. Jonah, while by no means *ugly*—ugliness is made up anyway, the part of her that has read too many online infographics reminds her—has never necessarily been the type of person who stands out in a crowd. She is broad-shouldered with a slouch, she is tired-eyed but too young to excuse it. The Creature that lives and grows inside of her head makes her stand up straight. It gives her a reason to look sickly. It touches her often, and its touch is the only one she finds herself able to stand these days.

The blue-haired phlebotomist asks Jonah about herself while tying up the latex tourniquet around her arm. She winces, but she tells them that she studied art history but that she works as a barista. They chat about neo-expressionism and the blood flows slowly into each vial, slower than it should, but that's normal by now. It's on her file and everything, so the phlebotomist doesn't question it, just taps their foot and stays on the topic of Basquiat's place in the canon. Once eight vials have been drawn and placed into a neat little holder, Jonah is given a bandage with smiley faces on it and a box of strangely vegetal apple juice. She's only started enjoying the taste recently, but she supposes that maybe she's just getting used to her reality.

Work is itself. Jonah gets too tired to stand for a few minutes, but shrugs it off when Diane, the too-hip forty-something who owns the café, asks her if she needs a break. Spite keeps her on her feet, as it often does. A customer cries about his girlfriend asking him to go on a break, and she gives him the almond milk he gets in his latte for free. "Maybe she means it," Jonah offers, with a smile that she knows probably looks more like a cringe, "Maybe in a week, things will be better?" and he looks down, shakes his head. His fat tears fall harder and harder onto the counter. Jonah plucks a leaf out of the back of her mouth and shoves it in her pocket, sanitizes her hands, and says, "I'll call you when your drink is done," as he heaves another sob out.

She wishes she could be angry at people like him, ones who can break down in public over things that aren't too frightening, but she can barely even muster up the energy to envy him for it. She wonders what she would even break down over when it comes down to it. She and the Creature are at a tentative piece, migraines and exhaustion aside, and she's living her life as she ought to.

She tilts her head to one side and hears the bones crack; the trellis that is her spine gets sore so easily these days. She hands the customer his drink and he sniffles as a teardrop hits her hand.

The second neurologist was called Dr. Black. Dr. Aker had sent Jonah to him after her second MRI showed roots growing out of her cerebellum. Dr. Aker had offered, "He'll handle this better than me," and a pursed-lip frown. The pursed-lip frown was a commonality between Dr. Black and Dr. Aker, though Dr. Black's frowns were far more frequently occurring, and tended to be closer to scowls.

In their first meeting, he had stated the obvious: "There is an organism of some sort living and growing in your brain."

"Can it be removed?" Jonah asked, which led to a biopsy, which led to what Dr. Black called, in his crackling voice, "A bit of a hydra situation," because the Creature responded to any sort of attempt at removal with almost exponential levels of growth. Attempts to *kill* the Creature with drugs and radiation were also ruled out after brief attempts.

Around this time, the *symptoms* started. There were already headaches, sure, but as the Creature grew and began to live more comfortably, Jonah was introduced to the exhaustion, the fainting, the nausea. Her vision was blurry even on her best days, one and a half of every little thing she saw unless she squinted. Her memory—already spotty on a good day—failed her often, she developed a tremor in her jaw, and, well, there was also the pain.

Jonah had dealt with pain before, of course. She had an ankle that liked to fall out of its socket, and she fell out of a tree when she was thirteen and fucked up her arm for much longer than it should've been fucked up. The pain the Creature caused was different than that or any other injury she'd ever sustained.

It was less an ache or a sting or a burn so much as it was a sudden awareness of everything inside of her. Each muscle, each organ, each bone would screamat her with the slightest movement or the slightest lack of movement. She thought through each and every heartbeat out of fear that it would just stop, felt each drop of stomach acid hit the mucus lining of her insides. Every nerve and synapse sang to her, one-million pinpricks and staticky buzzes at once.

Dr. Black had her journal about it, asked her for every gruesome detail. He'd touched her head and neck and stomach and legs and she started looking for another office that took her insurance.

※

Weed helps, a little bit. Not much, but Jonah takes it as an excuse to get high regardless. Her dealer is her high school ex, and the two of them have agreed to let the transaction occur in silence. Jonah has her med card, too, at Dr. Fuentetodos' suggestion, but she doesn't use it. She likes to pretend that this is for financial reasons.

In her apartment's living room, Jonah hands over three wrinkled twenties, and jumps as her ex touches her neck. "What the hell?"

"There's something on you. Thought it was a bug."

"Could've just told me."

Sunhwa puts her hands up, drops a baggie onto the table, and strolls out the door with a slow, frustratingly cocky sort of walk. Jonah's hands rush to her neck the second the door shuts, and she runs to the bathroom to see a tiny, dark sprout poking through. The spot around it is red and raw to the touch, and, despite herself, Jonah presses down on it so that it bleeds properly.

She thinks to herself, *this is what is supposed to happen*, until she thinks the opposite, and stops pressing on her neck, dripping now with blood as thick as sap. Her hand moves to wipe it off, and then it moves to her mouth, and the sweet, metallic taste soothes her mind before she panics.

Soon, the rest of it is gone, and all that remains is the sprout, which is a lighter, more verdant green now that it's clean of blood. She pulls out her phone and types an email to Dr. Fuentetodos, *hi I think the Creature is coming out. It is in my neck and it wants to be more. Please call.*

It is seven PM, though, so she doubts he will answer. She rips the smiley-face bandage off her arm and puts it into the trash bin. The gauze beneath it is bloody, and it falls to the ground before she can get it into the trash bin too.

The sprout extends itself sweetly until it becomes more of a tendril, and it brushes itself over her lips until she sighs, until she shuts her eyes, until she falls blissful.

Dr. Fuentetodos and Jonah's first meeting went extraordinarily well. They agreed to focus on symptom relief instead of removal, and he said that experiencing pain to that degree so often isn't sustainable. He was kind without too much pity, his touches were light and infrequent, and his hapless efforts to seem *cool* were earnest enough to be charming.

The pain quieted until it was more like white noise. Jonah decided that she could live like this. The Creature seemed to agree.

She wakes up on the bathroom floor with a warmth in her chest. Her phone—sticky blood covering the bottom of the screen—clock says it's seven forty. Not too much time out. It's hard to stand, so she doesn't. She stays on her back and knows that she will be better soon.

More tendrils have grown out from her neck, and they twist and wrap around her until they are blooming. Jonah wishes that she could tell what sort of flowers her body had been full of, but for all of these months, she'd never been able to identify them, and she still can't, not even with them right in front of her, planting themselves in her heart and her belly.

Blood has started to fill her mouth as leaves and needles of wood crawl through it, scraping her tongue and cheeks. She smiles and lets that saccharine ichor drip, drip drown as the Creature becomes her.

The tendrils grow thorns, the petals smell like heaven, and Jonah feels that familiar pain go from a drone to a symphony. She feels her heart convulse as vines crawl through its ventricles, feels her stomach hunger for more, more, until it is full of flowers and honey and until it is made whole.

She is aware of everything, and as she hurts, she laughs and laughs and laughs. The roots crawl over her face, and she leans into the touch, and feels so, so loved.

Acknowledgments

Thanks to:

My family, especially my parents.

My teachers and advisors—Dennis Nurkse, Neil Arditi, David Hollander, Jeffrey McDaniel, Mary LaChapelle, R.A. Villanueva, and Suzanne Hoover.

My dear friends: Arden Woods, Erin Coleman, Raven Miko Sato, Rupert Gilmer, Connor "Nye" Dexter, Camden Baker, Quill J. Park, and many, many more, with special thanks to Lee Beaudrot.

Robert Ottone and Michael Dolan, without whom this book would not have seen the light of day.

My tumors.

And everyone I have met who has ever died.

About The Author

Bee Hyland is a writer from Virginia who now lives in New York. Her creative and academic interests include illness, the sublime, parasitism, grief, and gender.